THIS BOOK BELONGS TO:

_____

DEDICATED TO ALL OF THE
WONDERFUL STUDENTS I HAVE
HAD THE PRIVILEGE OF TEACHING
AND MY BABY BOY WOODFORD.

WOODFORD THE DOG

WRITTEN BY:
ALYCIA EMERSON

WOODFORD THE DOODLE IS CUTE AS CAN BE.
HE IS COVERED IN GOLDEN FUR, YOU SEE.

HE ONLY WEIGHS JUST 50 POUNDS. HE HARDLY MAKES ANY SUDDEN SOUNDS.

WOODFORD LOVES TO RUN AND PLAY.
HE LOVES IT ANYTME OF DAY.

HE RUNS AROUND WITH ALL THE ZOOMIES. TO MAKE SURE THAT HE'S NEVER GLOOMY.

WOODFORD LOVES TO SHOW HIS MANY TRICKS. HE RUNS AND PLAYS FETCH WITH HIS STICKS.

HE KNOWS ALL OF THE PROPER COMMANDS. JUST LIKE SIT, STAY, AND STAND.

HIS FAVORITE TOY IS ALWAYS A BONE. WHEN HE CHEWS IT, HE'S IN THE ZONE.

He Loves To Chew Them Everyday. He Loves To Chew Them Every Which Way.

WHEN HE'S HAD ALL OF HIS FUN, THAT MEANS HIS DAY IS USUALLY DONE.

THEN HE CURLS UP IN A BALL. HE LOOKS SO VERY, VERY, SMALL.

OFF TO SLEEP, LITTLE WOODFORD GOES. HE SLEEPS WITHOUT ANY CARES OR WOES.

YOU CAN TELL THAT HE'S HAD SUCH A GOOD DAY. WOODFORD CAN'T WAIT TO WAKE UP AND PLAY.

ABOUT THE AUTHOR

As a new teacher during the pandemic in 2020, I was teaching my writing class to my 4th graders. We had just gotten our puppy, Woodford Quarantino Emerson, in April. I was teaching about creating a story and the elements that went into it. As I was doing that, I got this idea to write a book about Woodford! I kid you not, I sat in my classroom after school that day, and wrote this story about him. I had been dreaming about publishing a children's book for a while, so it was amazing that I was finally able to get a cool idea for a book! I had the best time writing this book, and I hope you all get to know and love Woodford, as much as we do.

ABOUT THE REAL WOODFORD

Woodford is a medium Goldendoodle. The story is based on Woodford's daily life and the things he enjoys. He loves to play and run with us. We go on hikes and take him to Starbucks for pup cups.

He loves to dress up for all the holidays and occasions. Currently, he wears his TCU collar to support the Horned Frogs, where my husband went to college. He also has a gold chain, pictured below, to match his Dad's chain.

Thank you for reading all about Woodford and supporting our dream to publish a Children's Book.